The Puck Hog

Volume 2

THE PUCK HOG

Volume 2

HAUNTED HOCKEY IN LAKE PLACID

by Christie Casciano

illustrated by Rose Mary Casciano Moziak

North Country Books, Inc
Utica, New York

ISBN-10 1-59531-040-1
ISBN-13 978-1-59531-040-8

Design by Zach Steffen & Rob Igoe, Jr.

Library of Congress Control Number: 2010036057

North Country Books, Inc.
220 Lafayette Street
Utica, New York 13502
www.northcountrybooks.com

To my sisters:
hockey coach Teresa
Marzec, Maria Magicaro,
Rose Mary Moziak, and
JoAnn Casciano. And
to my amazing mom,
Mary Casciano.
-Christie Casciano

To my sons, Christopher
and Daniel.
-Rose Mary Casciano Moziak

Foreword

Christie Casciano is one of a kind. Her viewers know her as a television newscaster on Syracuse station WSYR-TV. Christie's family knows her as a devoted mother of Joseph and Sophia. But The Hockey Maven knows her as someone who is about as nutty about the ice game as me—and that says a lot.

Having read *The Puck Hog* to my grandchildren, I can attest that it is a sweetheart of a story, and you don't have to be a hockey aficionado to appreciate it or find it a swell read.

But Christie has gone one better, and this book is it. Believe me, as an author I know that it's more than challenging to come up with two terrific books on the same subject, but she has pulled it off.

And if she does it again after this, that would make it an even better literary hat trick.

When asked what inspired her to pick Lake Placid as the venue, her response said it all:

"It was the location, not any particular person this time around, Lake Placid! It's such an inspirational place! The Miracle on Ice, what an inspirational story and moment in history.

"Our youth hockey experiences are also built into this story. Youth hockey has been an incredible journey for my family. Watching my children play, meeting so many great families, the dynamics of the game and our weekend adventures have all combined to awaken my creative writing soul!"

If I had one lasting impression from *The Puck Hog*, it was that I only wish it had been on the shelf of my local Brooklyn library when I was looking for a hockey book one winter's afternoon in 1939.

— *Stan Fischler, "The Hockey Maven," NHL Reporter & Hockey Analyst*

Chapter One

Ice chips flew in the cold heavy air, as the sound of hockey sticks hitting pucks echoed throughout the rink. Something was different about practice today. Sophia could not put her finger on exactly what it was. The drills were pretty much the same. Coach had them skate up the ice, side by side, pass to each other and shoot on the net. The ice had a solid, familiar feel. It had just been resurfaced and there were barely any bumps. The rough spot near the blue line that usually catches a blade and causes a thunderous face plant was perfectly patched.

What was so different? Sophia carefully looked around the rink. The net was in the same spot. Orange cones were carefully spaced

and zigzagged, ready to challenge speed and agility. The practice jerseys were a little bigger than last year's, but they were the same red, blue, green, and yellow colors that represented the lines for their offense and defense. Then it hit her.

"Hey, we're Squirts now!" she suddenly realized. Sophia glanced at her teammates to see if any of them were feeling the same morph moment. They were skating on the ice for the first time as Squirts. It was the next level in youth hockey, and it meant they were no longer the newbies.

"This year we are going to be skating against bigger, better, faster skaters," Sophia thought, and wondered, "Faster than Eddie? What if they're all just like Eddie? Imagine playing against a whole team of puck-hogging Eddies! Ugh!"

"Hey, what's with you?" Holden asked as he snuck up behind Sophia and angled his blades to stop just inches from her skates.

"Wow, Holden, really?" Sophia turned to Holden and gave him a stern look. "Our first day as Squirts and you're still acting like a mini-mite?"

Jamie slid from behind and whacked a puck between Sophia's skates. Holden caught the puck and snapped it back to Jamie as he quickly circled around Sophia.

"Okay, enough fooling around, guys!" Sophia spoke up loudly, "We're Squirts now, so no more kids stuff."

"Oh boy," Alec could not wait to jump in on this conversation as he placed his bulky, blue gloves on Sophia's padded shoulder. "Why do I feel another one of those blah, blah, blah moments coming on?"

Jamie gave Holden their secret signal. He raised his right glove up, and tapped his helmet three times. As Sophia began to lecture the boys about the difference in the level of play between Mites and Squirts, the two boys split up to get on opposite ends of the ice, then they raced full speed toward Sophia. When they were just a few feet away from her, they angled their just sharpened blades to shower Sophia. It was as if it was raining ice! Every inch of her was covered in thin, white shavings.

"We call it the Niagara Falls snow job," laughed Holden, "We've been practicing that move all summer, just for you!"

"Why do I even bother?" Sophia moaned.

"Okay people, now that you've had your little fun, let's focus," Sophia raised both arms in the air and started to brush the snow off her jersey.

"We're not Mites anymore guys. Next month, we're going to play in the Lake Placid tournament. My brother has been there and he says the teams are amazing. We might even play teams from Canada. Joe says the kids there are practically born with skates on their feet." Sophia's voice grew louder.

"Ouch," said Alec, "That's got to be painful for their mammas."

The giggles began and soon became uncontrollable. Even Sophia had to laugh at the thought.

"Okay," said Sophia, "Funny. But you get the point, right?"

"We get it," said Jamie, "We're going to Lake Placid. It's the holy land of hockey. There is gold in the hills of the Adirondacks!"

Eddie seemed to just appear out of nowhere, "Gold!" he exclaimed. "Another trophy for my trophy case, and another medal for my mantle."

"For all of our mantles, Eddie," Patrick said as he skated up to join the huddle, "I can see them. I can almost smell them."

"No," said Holden, "I think that's Eddie you smell. Whoa, Eddie, when was the last time you washed that jersey? You smell like a wet dog!"

"That stink," Eddie skated in a majestic manner toward his team-mates, "is a badge of honor. Don't you people know anything about the tradition of hockey?"

"Eddie," Sophia could not resist, "You really, really smell, and there's nothing honorable about that."

Chapter Two

Tweet! Tweeeeet! Tweeeeeeet!

The coach's piercing whistle sounded, signaling the start to their first practice as a Squirt team. The coach waved his big, black hockey gloves in the air, motioning everyone to gather around him. They quickly assembled and got down on one knee.

"Kids, I am so proud of all of you," Coach Paul said once he had their attention. "We're going to have another great year, just like we did last year. But this year is going to be a little different. You're going to be skating against bigger kids, so you've got to work on your speed and keep your head up. I am going to teach you a lot of ways to skate smart and avoid injuries. Safety is above everything when you play for me. After that, it's teamwork."

"Next month is going to be really exciting," the coach continued, smiling. "We will have our first tournament of the season and our first trip to Lake Placid. You'll be up against some of the best and toughest teams in the Northeast."

Cory spoke up, "Coach, Sophia's brother says we could play some Canadian teams too?"

"That's right," the coach continued, "But don't let that worry you. With the talent I've seen and the way you kids work hard and look out for each other, I know I'm going to be a very proud coach, no matter what the scoreboard says."

"Don't worry Coach," Eddie chimed in, "I'll be lighting the lamp and the scoreboard for you."

"Not for me," said Coach Paul, "for the team. And, don't forget..."

"I know, I know," moaned Eddie as he was suddenly joined by the entire team in saying, "Assists count just as much!"

Chapter Three

One week before the big Lake Placid tournament and the lines for the team were set. Sophia was on the red line, as a right wing, Holden was a left wing, and Eddie was their center. Jamie and Alec were assigned to play defense. All of the other lines, green, blue, and yellow, were strong too. The team members felt as if they could pass to each other with blindfolds on. With Tommy and Nick as their goaltenders, it seemed as if the team was right where it needed to be. But it was just about to get better.

"TWEEEET!"

The kids skated up and circled around the coach for what they thought was going to be another lecture about passing the puck.

"We only have three practices left before we head to Lake Placid," said the coach. "I thought we could use a little extra help."

"Oh, Coach," Justin moaned, "Not another long chalk talk about line changes. We get it now. We promise!"

"I know," said Michael, "You're going to make us watch the movie about the Miracle On Ice again, right?"

"No," said Christian, "I bet we're going to be working on our shots from the blue line. Mine is a cannon!"

The coach nodded, "All good stuff, kids. But, I've got something else planned."

From the corner of the rink, Sophia spotted a familiar purple and gold jersey, yellow helmet, and purple gloves slowly lifting the heavy bar that kept the door tightly shut. Her eyes widened and she smacked Holden on the shoulder and exclaimed, "Joe!"

Coach Paul smiled. "I thought some of the high school hockey players could skate with all of you and give you some pointers on what you need to do to have a good showing in Lake Placid. Ask them anything, and see if you can keep up with these big lugs."

"They're really going to skate with us?" Holden couldn't believe high school players would skate with Squirts. The high school boys, all seventeen of them, with their thickly padded shoulders, elbows, chests, and legs, stood more than six feet tall in their hockey skates. They looked like a field of giants next to their miniature counterparts.

The practice was exhausting. Everyone skated hard to impress and catch the attention of the high school kids. Eddie had no trouble keeping up with the bigger boys, even taunting them at times, saying "Just 'cause you're bigger, doesn't make you better!"

Sophia noticed Eddie quietly giggling and shaking his head up and down. "That's not a good sign," Sophia thought to herself, "It usually means he has something ridiculously annoying planned."

"Okay, Eddie," Sophia cornered him, "What are you up to?"

"Well," said Eddie, "Let's just say it's time to test out a little scientific theory."

"What theory, Eddie?" asked Sophia.

"Oh, you know the one about gravity? Plus the old saying, the bigger they are the harder they fall? MUAHA HAAA HAAA HAA," Eddie let out a long and evil laugh.

"What a weirdo," thought Sophia.

"Hey guys!" shouted Eddie to the high school boys. "Are you up for a little challenge? Remember this?" Eddie skated full speed toward the middle of the rink. When he reached center ice, he flopped on his belly and slid to the end of the ice in what's known in hockey as the Superman slide.

"Whoooo Hoooo!" Eddie roared loudly as he flew across the ice.

"Oh yeah," said Tyler. "I remember that. It's been awhile though."

The older boys lined up at the edge of the rink and took off. It was quite the site as the heavily padded teenagers took six quick, humongous strides, then plopped to the ice on their stomachs, their arms, chins, and feet raised up and stretched as far as they could go. They looked as if they were soaring in the sky. Their speed was incredible.

"Wow," Holden was amazed, "Look how fast they are flying across the ice.

"I wouldn't want to be in front of one of them!" shouted Michael.

"Oh no," screamed Sophia, "It looks like...."

Crash! Thump! Splat!

Their big bodies, one by one, bounced off the boards, and they all ended up flat on their backs.

"Good thing our pads are a lot thicker than when we were Squirts," groaned Joe, "because that could have really hurt."

"So much for being tough," Eddie let out another evil laugh as he snowed the motionless high school kids.

"Okay," said Tyler, "I've had just about enough of that kid. Guys, are you with me?"

The high school boys jumped up and tore after Eddie, who was at the corner of the rink.

"Aw, guys!" shouted Eddie, "I was just having a little fun."

Eddie was panicking; he felt like a bullfighter in a ring with seventeen angry bulls who were about to charge.

The boys skated full speed toward Eddie and blasted him with the biggest blade-created snowstorm anyone had ever seen.

"Whoa," said Holden, "That just made our Niagara Falls snow job look like Little Falls."

They moved away from their target. Eddie was buried. After about a minute, one of his black gloves emerged from the pile of white stuff. He was laughing hysterically. "Awesome. That was sooo cooool! Do it again!"

"Oh Eddie," said Sophia, "You're not just clueless, you're hopeless!"

Chapter Four

One last practice before the big game, and Coach Paul had one more inspirational trick up his sleeve.

"At tonight's practice," said Coach Paul to the team, "Guess what we're going to do?"

"Snow Eddie?" asked Holden.

"As much as we would all love to see that again, no," said their coach with a grin, "I thought we could use a little help from a big friend."

There was a curious look on the face of each member of the team, as their coach skated to the side of the rink to lift the heavy metal bar that kept the doors closed. Behind the glass, there was a really huge figure. They thought the high school kids were big, but this guy was monster-sized!

The coach slowly opened the large metal and glass door to reveal the surprise.

"What? No way! Seriously?" yelled the kids.

Then Sophia began to chant, and her teammates quickly joined in, "Crunchman! Crunchman! Crunchman!" they shouted as the big superhero joined them on the ice.

The mascot for the Syracuse Crunch doesn't talk. His lips are sealed with ice. The six foot caped crusader with wide eyes and super-sized hockey gloves doesn't need to say anything to get the kids pumped up. Music started to play. As he danced, Crunchman looked like he was made out of rubber. It didn't take long for the kids to skate over to fist bump the big mascot.

"He's here," said the coach, "because he wants to see you bring home the hardware. That means a trophy. To be placed in that case,"

the coach pointed to a large, glass trophy case that was just outside of the rink's main door. "The last team to bring home a Lake Placid trophy," said the coach as he pointed to Sophia, "Was your brother's team, Sophia."

"Joe says that was the dream team," Sophia recalled her brother talking about the year his team went to Lake Placid and won every matchup in the tournament. They pulled off a major upset against a Canadian team.

"Joe told me there was no secret to winning," Sophia said to the team, "Just work hard, work together, and have fun!"

"That's exactly what we're going to do, Sophia," said Coach.

Chapter Five

The road to Lake Placid was long and winding. As they got closer to their hotel in the village, Sophia noticed the mountains were taller and whiter.

"Are we there yet?" Sophia loudly whined.

"Okay," grumbled her dad, "Don't even start. This is a long drive. Please don't make it any longer."

"Sorry, Dad," Sophia pulled out her journal to document her journey, taking special note of the beautiful scenery. Joe had a stack of hockey magazines and books. One of his favorites was *Hockey Chronicle*, written by "The Hockey Maven," Stan Fischler. Joe admired the way Mr. Fischler could make the history of hockey come to life. He was determined to memorize tons of facts about his favorite players and dare anyone to quiz him.

After three long hours on the road, their SUV pulled into the parking lot of their hotel. The village was just as Sophia had imagined. It was charming, quaint, and so pretty.

"So here we are, where it all took place," Sophia turned to Joe.

Joe grinned. "Yes, this is where champions were crowned and history was made."

"So what are the chances of my team making some history, Joe, here in the land of the great?" asked Sophia.

"That all depends on how your team plays, Sophia. You know, they all need to show up," said Joe.

"Oh, well, that's no problem," Sophia responded. "Everyone is going to be here."

"No," said Joe," That's not what I mean by being there. Sometimes you can be on the ice, but not be in the game."

"Oh, I get it," said Sophia. "Like the time we played Auburn and we didn't play hard because we thought it was going to be an easy win. Boy, did we get a lesson in being overconfident. Then there was the time we got lazy playing Lysander's team. We barely won. Same thing happened when we played Skaneateles!"

"Exactly," said Joe. "You can't take anything for granted. Every time you step out onto the ice, you have to skate hard, work hard, and work with each other."

"So, Joe," Sophia continued her line of questioning, "If everyone does show up for this tournament with their heads in the game, what are our chances of winning it all?"

"Pretty good," said Joe, "Actually, really good. As long as you can stay out of the penalty box."

"Ha, ha," Sophia took her Syracuse Crunch hat off her head to give her brother a swift whack on his shoulder."

"Slashing!" Joe yelled, "In the penalty box, number eight!"

Chapter Six

The hotel lobby was filled with overstuffed hockey bags, and there was a long line of families waiting to check into their rooms. Sophia and Joe asked their parents if they could check out the pool, which was a tradition for the brother and sister.

"Fine," said their mom, "But I want you back here in 15 minutes."

Sophia and Joe gave their mom a blank stare and then pointed at the long line. Their mom stepped on her toes to look over the heads of the people in front of her and moaned as she said, "Okay, twenty-five minutes."

The pool looked so inviting. The water felt cool to the touch and the enclosed swimming area was steamy hot. The smell of chlorine permeated the air and tickled their noses. It was completely quiet; just one older couple swam gently across the pool, unaware of the two children watching them go back and forth.

"This scene is going to change, big time," said Joe, "when all your crazy little hockey buddies make their cannonball entrances into this pool and scream at the top of their lungs. It's going to be so loud in here, your ears are going to be ringing all night."

"Not tonight though," said Sophia, "Coach has a rule the night before our first tournament game. No swimming. Coach says swimming will make us skate like jellyfish."

"Good rule," said Joe, "Since you already look like one, it would be really bad if you skated like one too. Ha ha. I'm just playin' with you. All of my good coaches had the same rule."

"It stinks!" said Sophia. "Since we can't go swimming, what are we supposed to do? It is going to be really, really, really BORING."

"Boring?" Joe raised both eyebrows. "You don't get where you are. You're in Lake Placid, Sophia!"

"Come on," Joe motioned Sophia to follow him back to the lobby. As they walked, Joe reminded Sophia of all the fun they had during his tournament with his "dream team."

"Don't you remember all the cool Olympic T-shirts we bought in the shops in the village? Or that ice cream shop with forty-eight different flavors? The restaurants? Remember Mom taking you on that dogsled ride on Mirror Lake and you kept asking the musher, 'How do the dogs know when to stop?'"

"Oh yeah," Sophia smiled as she remembered bundling up on the sled, the barking dogs and the sound of the sled moving across the snow as it circled in a steady pattern on Mirror Lake.

"Don't forget," said Joe, "We can ride to the top of Whiteface Mountain in a gondola for a really cool view, or check out the Olympic speed skating oval and skate with history!"

As they walked toward the front desk, Sophia spotted her whole team hanging out in the lobby. It looked like they didn't know what to do either.

"Plus, the most fun of all, Sophia." Joe stopped and turned to her teammates as Sophia waited in anticipation, "Hey guys!" Joe shouted, "Grab your skates, sticks, and helmets and tell your parents to look right outside of that window."

Sophia looked out and saw a solid, frozen sun-glistening surface with a few figure skaters doing jumps and spins. They were skating on Mirror Lake!

"That," said Joe, "Is the ultimate skating experience! We're going to play some pond hockey, Sophia."

"Pond hockey?" Sophia's eyes widened as far as they could go and she crinkled her forehead, "Awesome!" Sophia had never skated on anything that didn't have a roof and wasn't surrounded by boards and Plexiglas.

The kids gathered their gear and flung their skates over their shoulders. Joe and some of the parents led them to the cleared patch on Mirror Lake.

The kids giggled when their blades hit the bumpy surface for the first time.

"Wow," said Holden, "This is amazing! Check this out!"

Holden waved his arms in the air and spun around. As he took a deep breath, his lungs felt the surprising sting of the cold air. The sounds were unique too—the crunching rhythm of skates carving turns in the diamond-hard ice. The kids used their boots for goal posts as they skated beneath a brilliant blue sky with no blue lines or face-off circles on a glimmering glass surface.

"Whoa!" Corey slipped and fell on his padded behind. "What's with this ice?"

"It's real ice!" shouted Eddie, "It's just like me. Rough and tough!"

"Okay," Joe interrupted, "Tone it down, hot shot. It just takes a little getting used to, Cory. Use your skills and you can skate on anything."

"Even the moon?" laughed Cory.

"Yeah, sure," Joe smiled as he shook his head.

Eddie held his hand up to his squinting eyes to block the glare of silver blades and white snow reflecting the bright sunshine. "Good thing I never leave home without these," Eddie bragged as he whipped a pair of sunglasses out of his front coat pocket. "Okay, losers, prepare to be dazzled by Eddie greatness."

Eddie did have some pretty amazing hockey skills, and even on the frozen pond, he had no problem stick handling and flying across a surface that was peppered with bumps and rough patches.

With no refs, no offsides, and no rules against cherry picking, the kids got to play the game the way it was meant to be played.

They fell a lot. But they laughed a lot too. Soon their cheeks turned bright red from the sun and wintry breeze as they raced for the puck on this rink with a magnificent view.

Chapter Seven

Back at the hotel, Sophia begged her parents to take them to the rink where the Miracle took place. It was only a few blocks away, so the family decided to walk. That was something Joe loved about Lake Placid. They could leave their car parked in the hotel lot and walk to the rinks, shops, and restaurants. There were so many great places to see and so much to do in this village nestled in the High Peaks region of the Adirondacks.

Squeek. Squeek. Slush. Slush. Thump! It was the sound of wheeled hockey bags hobbling across sidewalks and street corners.

"Why do parents buy those things for their kids?" an annoyed Joe loudly asked. "Real hockey players carry their bags."

"Wish I had one of those bags," moaned Sophia, as she thought about constantly struggling to keep the strap of her very heavy hockey bag on her shoulder. "It would be so much easier. Plus, they're so cool."

On the walk to the rink, they saw teams from all over the Northeast, many of them equipped with matching warm-up suits and hockey bags and sticks of the three hundred dollar variety. "Wow," said Sophia, "They look like NHL teams. I know you always say, Joe, that it's not how you look, it's how you play. But I still wouldn't mind looking sharp like that." Sophia pointed to a team of about twenty players, tall and stocky, in brightly colored jerseys— "Wow, they're so big."

Then, suddenly, they were there. There were so many flags surrounding the legendary 1980 Herb Brooks Arena, all standing at attention, waving gently in the soft breeze and brilliant sunshine. The building looked majestic to her; she just stared and stood there motionless.

"What's the matter honey?" asked her mom.

"Just give me a minute," said Sophia. "I've been waiting for this for a long time. For all nine years of my life."

"I know what you mean," said Joe, as he smiled and stared at the rink, "That's exactly how I felt the first time I stood before the Miracle on Ice Arena."

Chapter Eight

It was the day of the big game, and the family had decided to get an early start and check in at the rink two hours earlier than the scheduled start time. At the entrance, they found out Sophia's locker room number and the location of her game.

Sophia carefully looked at all of the old photos of hockey heroes of the past and their moments of glory. They lined the halls of the rink that held so many memories and hosted the Miracle. As they headed toward the locker room, Sophia turned the corner and her eyes met those of an old man. There was something about him that seemed out of place, but at the same time, as if he belonged, just like one of the trophies in the many trophy cases. He wore a blue jumpsuit and had a broomstick in his hands. But he held it like a hockey stick.

"Must be the janitor," Sophia turned to Joe.

"Who?" asked Joe.

"The man in that big trophy case," But when she pointed toward the floor-to-ceiling case, he was gone. Sophia shrugged her shoulders and hurried her pace, her heavy bag draped over her shoulder.

Sophia heard the sound of squeaky wheels quickly approaching from behind. She placed her bag down, but before she could turn around, she felt a sharp tug of her ponytail. "Do not touch the pony-tail, Eddie," Sophia quickly turned around to see Eddie, grinning from ear to ear, Christian by his side.

"What's up Sooo PHEEE ah? Hey, I just heard Coach is really uptight. He's pacing back and forth and talking about changing all the lines," said a panicked Eddie.

"I wonder why he's so nervous." said Christian.

"Well, let's not make it any worse. Let's get in the locker room."

"I just need to grab my gear, and I'll be right in," said Sophia. Sophia turned around to grab her hockey bag and there he was again. The janitor was inside the trophy case, polishing the biggest trophy there. "Odd," she thought to herself, "How did he get in there?" There wasn't a door, just a sliding glass window that opened the case. She bent down to pick up her bag and when she looked up, he was gone again. "How does he do that?"

Once the whole team was gathered in the locker room, the Coach announced he was going to change the lines.

"Sophia," he said, "Anish has an upset stomach, so I'm going to need you to be on defense. You know how he gets when his stomach is aching. "

"Oh, come on, Coach. Just 'cause his legs get all wobbly? He'll be fine," said Sophia. "I don't want to play D."

"Sorry, Sophia," said the coach, "But when Anish's legs get all wobbly, he can't skate backwards. You can't play D if you're not going to skate backwards."

"Okay," Sophia sighed. She dropped her head down, holding back her tears. She had wanted her first skate on the history-making ice to be as a forward.

"Also everybody, watch out," said the coach. "They've got some kids who take some pretty cheap shots, so keep your head up and try to avoid the corners if you see them coming after you."

Holden turned to Jamie, who was always doing research on the teams they were playing. "What did you find out about these guys?"

"They play dirty," said Jamie. "Coach is right. They've got a couple of cheap shot artists on the team. When I saw them play in Buffalo, they flattened this one kid so badly, he got carried out of the rink on a stretcher."

"Whoa," said Holden. "How do they get away with that?"

"They also have a couple of puck hogs on the team, so they don't play together at all. They're all out for themselves. I think we can beat 'em."

As the team skated out onto the 1980 rink for warm-ups, a feeling of pride, joy, and nervousness embraced them. Sophia looked up at the stands and saw her parents. She gave them a quick wave, and then she noticed the janitor was a few rows behind them. He didn't have a broomstick in hand. He had a hockey stick, and he was wearing a jersey that looked a lot like theirs. "Guess we've got a fan," Sophia smiled to herself.

The game was pretty brutal, and it got even uglier in the last period. Alec had a breakaway, and he was about to enter their zone when he spotted two huge defenseman making their way right at him. He moved the puck to the corner, and just as everyone had feared, they smooshed him like a sandwich. Alec went down hard. The whistle blew, and his teammates' hearts stopped. Alec wasn't moving. Coach and Joe hurried to his side. It seemed like he was down for a very long time. Everyone got down on one knee and waited, hoping he was okay. With help from Coach and Joe, Alec slowly got up. The players tapped their sticks on the ice and spectators in the stands applauded as he hobbled off the ice. The ref called the penalty. Both players from the other team were sent to the penalty box.

"Good," said Christian, "They're gone."

"Yeah," said Anish, "Time to get even."

Joe responded sternly to Anish and the whole team, "Look. We're not going to play their game, guys. Yes, we'll get even, but on the scoreboard. Calm down and focus on teamwork."

"Listen up team," Coach called a time out. "I've got an idea." The coach pulled out his white board and outlined a new game plan.

The plan worked beautifully. Sophia was rock solid on defense, and so was Alec, who had insisted on getting back into the game. Holden and Eddie worked extra hard to get the puck to the net. In the final minutes of the game, Eddie passed the puck to Holden.

Holden made a beautiful backhand shot over the goalie's glove. It was the most glorious goal Holden had ever scored. The victory was sweet. The team went on to achieve back to back wins, and they made it to the championship round. They were going to face the big and much-feared Canadian team.

Chapter Nine

The night before the big game, Coach Paul made a list of rules for all of the players to follow. No swimming. No sweets. No skiing. No snowboarding.

"No snowboarding? WHAAT??" Eddie was stunned. "This is not going to fly with my dad!" exclaimed Eddie. Eddie was an excellent snowboarder. His dad was training him for a big competition right before Christmas. He had a real good shot at winning a medal because he was very close to landing a new maneuver called the rodeo flip.

Eddie showed the list to his father. "We're in Lake Placid, Dad. There's no way we're going to pass up on a chance to slide down one of the best snowboarding mountains on the planet!"

"You got that right," Eddie's father placed his hand on his shoulder. "Give me that list."

He grabbed the list from Eddie and tore it up into tiny little pieces, letting the pieces fall to the ground, "Those rules are for other kids. Not my champion."

That afternoon, Eddie and his father headed to Whiteface Mountain. As usual, his father gave him a lecture before he took his first run. "You need to work on your timing, Eddie," said his dad. "You're so close to landing your rodeo flip. If you land it, with all your other tricks, you're a guaranteed gold medal winner."

"Got it, Dad,"

Eddie's father followed behind on skis. The conditions were perfect, and Eddie was feeling confident. He went up in the air, flipped, and was so close to a perfect landing. But instead, Eddie tumbled down hard.

His father rushed to Eddie and began to yell, "Timing. Timing, Timing! You just don't pay attention!"

"Dad," Eddie moaned, "My wrist. It really, really hurts,"

Eddie's dad rolled his eyes, "What now? You can't seem to get anything right these days. Now get up!"

Eddie stood up and held his wrist, "Dad, I'm trying to tell you, my wrist hurts. A lot."

"Shake it off!" yelled Eddie's dad, "Quit acting like a baby!"

He angrily waived his arms "You know what? Let's just call it a night!"

Eddie pulled his jacket up to the tip of his eyes and buried his face in his zipper. He didn't want his dad to see his tears.

When they got back to the hotel, his dad filled a sandwich bag with ice and handed it to Eddie. "Still hurt?" his dad asked him.

"Yeah. A lot. I can't play tomorrow," said Eddie.

"Excuse me? Did I just hear you say you can't play?" His face was red and his eyes filled with anger, but Eddie's dad calmly said, "Okay. Let me look at that wrist." Eddie's dad examined his son's wrist, and there was no swelling or bruising.

"Does it hurt here?" as he gently pressed on Eddie's wrist.

"Yeah. Ouch,"

"It looks fine. Well, one way to find out." His dad got Eddie's hockey stick. "Here. Grab your stick."

Eddie reached for the stick, but was unable to tightly grip it, "No dad. I can't. I'm telling you I can't play. It really hurts."

"Fine," said Eddie's dad. "I've had enough. I'm calling your coach. You'll be in the stands tomorrow watching your team lose. Keep ice on it. Go to bed."

Chapter Ten

Word about Eddie's injury spread to the team. He was lying down feeling sorry for himself when he heard a knock at his door.

"Go away!" he shouted.

Eddie's mom answered the door and saw the whole team.

"Eddie," said his mom, "I think you're going to want to see this."

One by one, the team walked into the hotel room, each of them carrying a hockey stick with a balloon tied to the end. Each balloon had a message for Eddie: "We need you!" "Eddie you rock!" "Beat Canada!" "Feel better!"

"So, the time it took for all of you to blow up all these balloons and write on them, you could have been out on the ice, practicing for the big game."

"No way, teammate," said Sophia, "We weren't going to leave you out, no matter what."

"One for all, and all for one!" the whole team shouted.

"Guys, thanks, and I'm sorry. I really messed up," Eddie said, his eyes focused on the floor.

"Are you still coming to the game tomorrow?" asked Holden.

Eddie's dad, who had just walked into the room, quickly answered, "He'll be watching from the stands. He's not going to mess that up."

"Poor Eddie," Sophia thought to herself, "His dad sure is mean."

"Mr. Easton?" Sophia walked up to Eddie's father, "The coach wanted me to tell you he's going to keep Eddie's name on the roster. Coach says, after all, we are playing on the Miracle On Ice arena," Sophia said with a hopeful look in her eyes.

"Well," said Eddie's dad, "That's the coach's decision. Better tell him not to hope for any miracles."

Chapter Eleven

The next morning, the team headed to the rink with mixed emotions. They were nervous without Eddie, but excited they made it to the championship round.

As she walked down the hall, Sophia noticed the janitor was in the case again, with his rags and polish. "Boy, he really makes sure no dust collects on that trophy. Wonder who he will be rooting for today?" Everyone else was too busy thinking and talking about the game to notice him there.

Sophia dressed quickly, then asked the coach if she could fill her water bottle. A drinking fountain was just outside the door of the locker room.

As she was filling her bottle, she heard a deep voice say, "Heard your team had a tough break."

She looked up. It was the janitor.

"Boy, you're not kidding," Said Sophia. "How did you hear?"

"Word travels fast when you're the team to beat."

"What's your name, sir?"

"Argus."

"Argus? That's an unusual name. Are you the janitor here?"

"I like to think of myself as the caretaker."

"Well, Mr. Argus, if you care anything about rooting for the winning team, you better find another jersey to wear," Sophia's chin dropped to her chest.

"You're never going to win, going into a game with that kind of an attitude," said Argus. "A long time ago, no one thought my team would have a sliver of a chance at beating one of the toughest teams that ever hit the ice. I was handed a note from a man who

spent a lot of time at our rink, and what that note said turned our game around. I've handed it to a few other team leaders over the years. Maybe it's time to part with it again. Here. But don't read it until it's time."

Sophia took the folded note and turned toward the locker room door because the coach was blowing his whistle. She turned around to Argus to ask him what he meant and how she was supposed to know when it was time to read the note. He was gone again.

She hurried to the locker room where she folded the paper into her glove.

The coach gave everyone a pep talk before the game. Eddie was in the stands with his parents, and the coach told them to play for Eddie, and to skate fast and beat them to the puck, like Eddie would.

The game's first two periods were the most exhausting they had ever played; they were never in the lead. In the stands, Eddie watched in silence. Parents kept coming up to him saying how sorry they felt for him, and how he would have made a big difference out there.

"They're right, you know," said Eddie's dad. "You're a real talent, son. You're also a good teammate. To your credit, you've become a leader. You can really motivate everyone. You really care about your teammates. I agree with everyone—you really would have made a big difference out there."

"You really mean that?" asked Eddie.

"I really do," Eddie's dad put his arm around his son's shoulder.

"Dad," there was a long pause, "I...I have something to tell you," Eddie swallowed hard and sighed, "My wrist doesn't really hurt. I was faking because I was afraid of disappointing you. I didn't want to let you down again. Please don't be mad at me."

Eddie's father looked down and shook his head.

"I am not surprised," said Eddie's dad, "Your mom suspected that's what was going on. She kept warning me that I've been pushing you too hard. It's just that I want to see you succeed where

I've failed. I never made it to the NHL, never won that ski trophy, and you're so much more talented than I ever was. I've failed at everything. Now, I've even failed at being a dad. I'm sorry."

Eddie's father paused, "If you want to go out there, I need to be sure you're wrist is okay. But we don't have a hockey stick for me to test you."

"No, but I can prove it to you, Dad. Give me your hand." Eddie held his hand out, and waited for his father to extend his hand. Eddie grabbed his dad's rugged hand and squeezed tightly. "I've been working on my tight grip. Dad, I love you."

"I love you too, son," Eddie and his dad held on tightly for another couple of minutes, and then his father put his hand under his son's chin, and looked him in the eyes, "Now, how about you go in that locker room and suit up. Go out....and..."

"I know. I know," said Eddie, "Go out and score."

No, said his dad, "Go out and have fun."

Chapter Twelve

It was the end of the second period and time for the ice to be resurfaced. Both teams headed to their locker rooms, and Eddie's dad caught Coach Paul in the hallway to tell him the good news about Eddie.

"Good thing you kept him on the roster, Coach, and I'm sorry," he said.

"I know you just wanted what's best for him," said Coach Paul, "We're glad to have him back."

In the locker room, everyone was tense and nervous. Behind by a goal the entire game, the team was able to tie it up in the last second, but was out of gas and losing confidence.

"Well," said Christian, "At least we didn't lose too badly."

"I know," said Holden, "We held them in that last period. I just don't think I've got anything left in me anymore. I'm beat."

Suddenly, the door to the locker room swung open, and an annoying and familiar voice yelled out, "What's up, Eddie wannabes?"

The team looked up and couldn't believe their eyes. Eddie? He was dressed and ready to play.

"What about your wrist?" asked Holden.

"I've been cleared to play. So you got me, if you still want me. I'm good to go. So, let's go get 'em!"

"Awesome!" shouted the team.

When there was only one minute left in the period, their coach decided to pull Nick, the goalie, out of the net to give them an extra player on the ice.

"Eddie, we are going to have you play center, but they're going to expect you to have the puck. We want to fake them out. Pass the puck to Jamie, and then skate like the wind. Sophia, you position yourself right near the net and get ready if there's a rebound. Alec, Cory, and Justin, you guys need to try to get the puck in their zone too."

"Coach, I'm not sure about this, said Eddie. "We've never done this play before."

Sophia remembered the note Argus handed her. She pulled it out of her glove and handed it to Eddie.

"What's this?"

"I'm not sure. Read it."

Eddie opened the note and then let out a mischievous laugh.

"Okay, I'm ready. One goal needed to win this thing. Let's do it!"

Eddie got the puck and dug his edges into the ice. He passed the puck to Jamie, who got it to the corner of the ice, and then passed it to Eddie who was center ice. Eddie had a clear path to the net, when suddenly he spotted a huge defenseman coming right at him. He slipped his stick back and watched the puck glide and slide perfectly to the bright purple tape on Sophia's stick. Sophia was right in front of the net. She slid her stick back and she went top shelf. She found the spot where grandma hid the cookie jar. The buzzer sounded. Game over.

"Winning goal scored by number 8!" shouted the ref.

The coach yelled from the bench, "Great job, Eddie and Sophia!"

The whole team copied Eddie's signature celebration. They all made a fist and got down on one knee as they slid across the ice. "We did it! We did it!" shouted Alec. "Oh yeah, weeee are the CHAAAMPIONS," sang Jamie. Then Christian chimed in, "It's another Miracle on Ice!" "Our very own Miracle!" shouted Micheal.

They lined up and shook hands with the Canadian team, "Good game, good game," they said as they bumped gloves down the line. Then it was time to celebrate the monumental win in a monumental way. The team dogpile!

One by one, they got up from their human tower and noticed all the camera lights flashing. The kids felt like rock stars. "Got to love the parent paparazzi," laughed Alec as he turned and posed for each and every camera lens.

In the locker room, Sophia couldn't wait to ask Eddie, "Hey, Eddie. What did that note say?"

"You mean, you don't know? Well, it said grandma's cookie jar. When I saw that, I knew exactly what to do. You're the only one on the team who can make that top shelf shot. That goalie couldn't stop anything top shelf. So, I knew I had to pass the puck to you, instead of trying to take a shot myself. So, where did you get that note?" asked Eddie.

"Long story," said Sophia.

Chapter Thirteen

Pizza party and swimming plans were being made by the coach and parents. Sophia could not wait to see Argus to thank him for the note of inspiration.

Sophia met her brother and parents in the hall and told them she wanted them to meet a friend. She looked down the hallway and in the trophy case, but there were no signs of Argus.

She saw a rink guard at the entrance and decided to ask him where he might be.

"Excuse me, sir?" Sophia looked up at the rink guard. "I'm looking for the janitor. He's kind of tall, carries his broom like a hockey stick, and his name is Argus."

"Argus? Did you say Argus? You actually saw him?"

"Yeah, Argus, or Mr. Argus," said Sophia.

The guard looked stunned.

"That name is a legend around here. But the only ones who have ever seen him, or claimed to have seen him, were the captain of the 1932 team and the coach of the 1980 team."

"WHAT?" Sophia was stunned.

"Yes, crazy isn't it? So, you say you've seen this Argus fellow? Or did someone tell you that a lot of people believe Argus is the reason that coveted miraculous trophy is in that case?"

Sophia looked at the case, and she thought she had caught a glimpse of the old man's twinkling eyes. But it was just a brilliant ray of sunshine that had reflected off the trophy.

"Funny," said the rink guard. "Wow. Never seen the trophy shine quite like that before. Did someone put a light in that case?"

"No light," said Sophia, "It just has a very good caretaker."

About the Author

Christie Casciano Burns, a television news anchor in Syracuse, New York, had no idea how much her life would change the first time her son picked up a hockey stick. From that point on, she and her husband, John, would find themselves spending many hours watching their children develop their hockey skills. They now shuttle their two skaters, Joe and Sophia, to games and practices at rinks throughout New York State. Like so many other hockey parents, when not in the stands, you'll find Christie volunteering at hockey games, tournaments, and fund-raisers.

Christie is a graduate of Syracuse University's S.I. Newhouse School of Public Communications. She has been a reporter and anchor for WSYR-TV since 1986. She also provides morning news updates for the popular B104.7 country radio station. Christie often volunteers as a celebrity reader at local schools and has hosted events to encourage children to read. She also writes a monthly column for *USA Hockey Magazine*.

You can follow Christie throughout the hockey season on her Syracuse Hockey Mom's Network, www.thepuckhog.blogspot.com, and become a fan on Facebook!

About the Illustrator

Rose Mary Casciano Moziak is an advertising designer for Spirit and Sanzone Distributors and a freelance artist. She received a Bachelor of Fine Arts degree from Syracuse University. Rose Mary lives in Fayetteville, New York, with her husband Don and two sons, Christopher and Daniel.

About the Syracuse Crunch

The 2012-13 season marks the Crunch's 19th year in Central New York. The Crunch joined the AHL for the 1994-95 season and have had primary affiliations with the Vancouver Canucks (1994-2000), the Columbus Blue Jackets (2000-10), the Anaheim Ducks (2010-2012) and the Tampa Bay Lightning (beginning in 2012-13).

The Crunch made history by hosting the first-ever AHL outdoor game (Mirabito Outdoor Classic) during the 2009-10 season, setting an AHL all-time attendance record in the process (21,508).

The Crunch play their home games at the War Memorial Arena in downtown Syracuse, NY. You can follow the Crunch by visiting the club's official website, www.syracusecrunch.com.

A Message From Crunchman About Bullying

Sophia made a great play to help win the big game, but what makes her the team's real hero?

Hockey is a fun sport, especially when players work together and support each other. Sophia had the courage to speak up to Eddie about being a puck hog. She helped him understand that teamwork is what makes hockey fun, not just scoring goals.

Celebrating with your teammates is fun, but putting down others is not. On the ice or off the ice, there is no place for a bully. If you see someone being disrespectful, will you have the courage to speak up? You can be a hero like Sophia by standing up to bullies and doing the right thing.